The
Magical Adventures
of Krishna

How a Mischief Maker
Saved the World

Vatsala Sperling

Illustrated by Pieter Weltevrede

Bear Cub Books
Rochester, Vermont • Toronto, Canada

For Dada, Harish Johari

Bear Cub Books
One Park Street
Rochester, Vermont 05767
www.InnerTraditions.com

Bear Cub Books is a division of Inner Traditions International

Text copyright © 2009 by Vatsala Sperling
Art copyright © 2009 by Pieter Weltevrede

LIBRARY OF CONGRESS CATALOGING-IN-PUBLICATION DATA

Sperling, Vatsala.
  The magical adventures of Krishna : how a mischief maker saved the world / Vatsala Sperling ; illustrated by Pieter Weltevrede.
    p. cm.
  ISBN 978-1-59143-110-7 (hardcover)
  1. Krishna (Hindu deity)—Childhood—Juvenile literature. I. Weltevrede, Pieter, ill. II. Title.
  BL1220.S66 2009
  294.5'2113—dc22
                                                                    2009025639

Printed and bound in India by Replika Press Pvt. Ltd.

10   9   8   7   6   5   4   3   2   1

Text design and layout by Virginia Scott Bowman
This book was typeset in Berkeley with Apple Chancery and Abbess as display typefaces

To send correspondence to the author of this book, mail a first-class letter to the author c/o Inner Traditions • Bear & Company, One Park Street, Rochester, VT 05767, and we will forward the communication.

Cast of Characters

Vishnu ('Vish-noo)
Lord of Preservation; also called Narayana, which means "born from the Original Man"

Lakshmi (Lack-shmee)
Lord Vishnu's wife, Goddess of Wealth

Shesha ('Shay-sha)
Lord Vishnu's serpent

Krishna ('Krish-nah)
Incarnation of Lord Vishnu on Earth; his name means "midnight blue"

Radha ('Raad-'haa)
Krishna's girlfriend, incarnation of Goddess Lakshmi on Earth

Balaram ('Bala-rahm)
Krishna's cousin, incarnation of Shesha on Earth

Bhumi ('Boo-mee)
The earth goddess; appears as a cow

Kansa ('Kahn-sa)
Powerful demon king; Krishna's uncle

Yogamaya (Yohg-'my-a)
Goddess of Illusion; appears as the fierce goddess Durga

Devaki (Day-vah-'kee)
Kansa's sister; Krishna's mother

Vasudeva (Vah-soo-'day-vah)
Devaki's husband; Krishna's father

Yashoda (Yah-'sho-da)
Krishna's adoptive mother

Narada ('Nah-rah-da)
A wise sage

Trinavrata (Trin-'ah-vra-ta)
A demon who appears as a whirlwind

Vatasura (Vah-'tah-soor-a)
A demon who appears as a calf

Bakasura (Bock-'ah-soor-a)
A demon who appears as a bird

Aghasura (Agh-'ha-soor-a)
A demon who appears as a serpent

Akrura (Ah-'kroor-a)
A wise devotee of Lord Vishnu

About Krishna

The Hindu people from India believe that whenever the earth is taken over by evil, the prayers of the weak will be heard by Lords Brahma, Vishnu, and Shiva (gods of creation, preservation, and destruction). Then the gods will work together to restore order and peace.

An ancient text in the Sanskrit language, the Srimad Bhagavatam, describes one such event from thousands of years ago. It tells the story of a time when demons ruled the world, led by the evil demon king Kansa. The gods decided that Vishnu should go to Earth to defeat Kansa and his cronies.

So Vishnu was born on Earth as a baby boy named Krishna. In his childhood, Krishna was a fun-loving and curious boy. He loved to play tricks on the village milkmaids, stealing the butter pots right off their heads. And he played the flute so beautifully that he enchanted all who heard him. But as carefree and childish as he seemed, Krishna was always on the lookout for demons, bravely killing any that crossed his path.

Whatever he did, Krishna acted with such flair, charm, playfulness, and humor that the stories of his many adventures continue to entertain and inspire us even today.

The northern plains of India, below the majestic Himalaya Mountains, were very fertile at one time. The great river Yamuna began her journey in the icy peaks of the Himalayas and ran through the northern plains on her way to the ocean, nourishing the soil as she flowed. On the banks of the Yamuna, several villages nestled in an endless expanse of wild, green woods and lush, rolling meadows. Amid such beauty and splendor, the citizens of Mathura herded cattle and lived quite prosperously.

But everything changed when the demon Kansa became king of Mathura. Kansa commanded a great empire, but he ruled his subjects with an iron fist and evil intentions. His greed for wealth was insatiable. To fill his royal coffers, he taxed the poor villagers very harshly. When people could not pay up, he sent his fierce demon messengers to punish them. Wherever these demons went, chaos and destruction followed. They demolished whole villages, killed children, stole cattle, and set fire to standing crops. They stopped at nothing, and the people got the message loud and clear, "Pay your taxes or else!"

It soon became impossible for people to keep up with the unjust demands of their cruel king. They knew that Kansa had imprisoned his own father, the kind and generous king Ugrasena, simply because the old king had objected to his son's ruthless greed. The people had no one to turn to. In desperation, they looked to the heavens and prayed to Lord Vishnu, saying, "Please help us, Narayana."

Another cry for help to the people came from the earth goddess, Bhumi. Bhumi was very generous. She gave her rich soil and flowing waters freely so that all the people could prosper. But no matter how she tried, Bhumi could not produce enough wealth to satisfy Kansa's greed. She knew that the people lived in terror of their king. No matter how hard they worked, they could never fill Kansa's bottomless coffers. Bhumi felt helpless as she watched the innocent people suffer.

When she could bear no more, she took the form of a cow and went to the heavens to seek help from Lords Brahma and Shiva. Lord Brahma had created Kansa. Lord Shiva would know how to destroy him. The gods listened to Bhumi's tale of woe. After some deep thinking, they said, "Only Narayana can help in these hard times, Bhumi. Let's go see him."

Soon they arrived at Lord Vishnu's home in the Ksheer Sagar, an ocean of milk that nourished the entire creation. Vishnu bobbed gently on the waves of milk, resting on the back of his great serpent, Shesha. The five-headed serpent made a magnificent coil and spread out his hoods. His ten beady eyes shone like jewels and five red tongues leaped out of his mouths like flames from a roaring fire pit. Lord Vishnu's wife, the goddess Lakshmi, sat beside him on the serpent's back.

Bhumi bowed humbly to Lord Vishnu. "Help us, Narayana," she cried. "Kansa, the cruel demon king, has made life impossible for the people. No one feels safe anymore." Bhumi's eyes stung with hot tears and her voice quavered as she begged for Lord Vishnu's help on Earth.

"Don't worry," he comforted Bhumi. "I will be born on Earth as Krishna to teach those demons a lesson." Patting Shesha, Vishnu said, "On Earth, you will be my cousin Balaram." Then he winked at his wife and said, "Sweetheart, I cannot live without you. You will be my girlfriend Radha."

Bhumi sighed with relief, because she knew that Lord Vishnu would keep his word.

In the whole world, the one person Kansa loved dearly was his little sister, Princess Devaki. He had just attended Devaki's marriage to Vasudeva, the king of a clan of cowherds. After the wedding, Kansa drove the newlyweds' chariot, whistling a merry tune and urging the handsome horses on. The starry-eyed couple waved to the people who had come out in droves to greet them. All of a sudden, a booming voice spoke from the sky. "Beware, Kansa! Your dear sister, Devaki, will have eight sons and the eighth will be the death of you."

A hush fell over the jubilant crowd. Kansa's face froze. He looked around. Raising his proud head to the heavens, he said in a voice as loud and booming as the voice from above, "There will be no Devaki! She will have no eighth son!"

In a flash, he jumped out of the chariot. His cruel, steely eyes blazed bloodred as he grabbed Devaki by her long hair, dragged her out of the chariot, and took a sword to her neck.

Vasudeva was horrified. He cried, "O King, is this any way to treat your dear sister on her wedding day? She is innocent. Let her go! I promise that I will give you our eighth child."

Kansa knew that Vasudeva would keep his word. He let go of Devaki and sheathed his sword. But instead of driving the newlyweds to their royal palace, he locked them up in a fortress dungeon on the banks of the Yamuna River. His father, King Ugrasena, was jailed there as well.

There is really no need to kill my beloved little sister, thought Kansa. *But her eighth child will not live to see the light of day! Anyway, I'm safe until she delivers her eighth son.*

In due time Kansa learned that Devaki had given birth to her first baby boy. He thought nothing of it. But Sage Narada, a holy man devoted to Lord Vishnu, visited Kansa's palace soon after the baby was born. He held a lotus flower in his hand. "Look at this flower, Kansa. Tell me which is the first petal and which is the eighth?" he asked with a sly grin.

Kansa thought for a moment. He knew that Sage Narada's questions always pointed to a hidden meaning. Something clicked in Kansa's devious mind. He threw the flower down and marched straight into Devaki's prison cell. Snatching the baby from her lap, he flung the child against the wall, killing him instantly. Devaki fainted and fell to the floor, while Vasudeva looked on, frozen in horror. "You must give me all of your sons, not just the eighth one," Kansa ordered Vasudeva. He turned on his heel and marched out of the prison.

Sage Narada saw it all, and smiled knowingly. He knew that Lord Vishnu had seen everything, too. The crueler Kansa became, the sooner Lord Vishnu would come to Earth.

Every year Devaki gave birth to a baby boy. Every baby met his end soon after he was born. Devaki's tears had dried up. She lived in a daze. With each and every breath she prayed, "Please help us, Narayana,"

Lord Vishnu heard each of her prayers. When he felt that Devaki could hold on no longer, he summoned Yogamaya, the goddess of illusion. "I am going to Earth to be born as Devaki's eighth son. I need you to come to Earth, too, to help me play a trick on Kansa. Go to the home of Nanda and Yashoda on the banks of the Yamuna River, and take birth as their baby girl."

Yogamaya knew to say, "Yes, Sir."

It was the eighth night after the dark moon in the month of August. Monsoon rains had just begun on the plains of northern India. The night sky, dark as ink and laden with black, ominous clouds, was lit every now and then with a bright, blinding streak of lightning. Rolling thunder made it impossible to hear anything. Throughout the day and night rains had come in great torrents, causing flash floods in the city of Mathura and swelling the river Yamuna where it flowed just outside the prison gates. The night was scary and dark. The river was deep and wild.

Within the prison walls, Devaki gave birth to her eighth son. She named him Krishna for he was as dark as the night outside. She raised the newborn to her lips to kiss him before Kansa took him away. Just then she noticed something strange—a halo around the baby's head! She whispered to Vasudeva, "Look! Look at our baby . . ." and they saw that in his tiny hands the baby held a little conch shell, a mace, a discus, and a lotus flower—the four sacred objects of Lord Vishnu! They wondered aloud, "Could our baby be Lord Vishnu?"

In answer, the baby spoke. "Mother, Father, this is not the first time I have come to Earth, and it will not be the last. I come to protect the innocent every time the earth is taken over by evil. Quickly now, take me to Nanda and Yashodas' home. They will raise me as their own. And bring their daughter back with you."

The next moment, the four sacred objects disappeared from the baby's hands and he became a helpless newborn again, squirming to find his thumb. Vasudeva noticed that his shackles had fallen to the floor. The lock on the gate had broken open, as if by magic, and the guards had fallen sound asleep. Quickly, he gathered some rags, wrapped the baby snugly, laid him in a basket, and stepped outside.

Vasudeva knew that Nanda and his wife Yashoda lived in Gokul, a little village
just across the river from the prison, but to get there he had to cross the raging
floodwaters. "Help me please, Narayana," he said, as he stepped into the river,
holding the baby high above his head. The water flowed right up to his chin and
he struggled against the powerful current. But just then the river water touched
one of Krishna's tiny toes and immediately the flood began to subside. A clear path
opened up right in front of Vasudeva and a snake came slithering behind him,
spreading its mighty hood over the baby to protect him from the downpour.

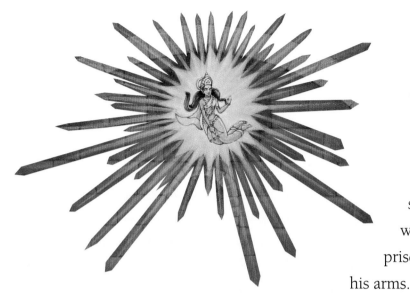

In Nanda's house, his wife, Yashoda, was fast asleep after giving birth to a baby girl. Very quietly, Vasudeva tiptoed to Yashoda's bedside, swapped the babies, and walked all the way back to the prison, cradling her daughter in his arms.

In the morning Kansa got news of the birth. *I will waste no time in getting rid of the baby,* he thought, and he marched right over to Devaki's cell.

"Please spare this one child, Brother, she's a little girl!" cried Devaki. Kansa hesitated for a moment. *Maybe there's nothing to the prediction,* he thought. *The eighth child is supposed to be a boy. . . .* Then fearing some trick, he roughly snatched the baby from his sister's frail arms. But as he tried to fling her against the wall, the baby girl slipped right out of Kansa's hands. She floated to a high spot on the ceiling beyond his reach and said, "Kansa, your killer is in Gokul." Startled, Kansa looked up and saw that the baby was none other than Yogamaya, who had disguised herself as the fearsome goddess Durga to give him a really good scare. Pale and shaken, he fled from the cell.

In Gokul, Nanda and Yashoda woke up in the morning and saw an unusually dark-skinned baby boy in their bed. "I thought I had given birth to a baby girl," Yashoda said to herself. But the next moment her doubt had vanished and she was flooded with an immense feeling of love for her new baby boy.

Little Krishna grew to be an adorable child, always smiling and gurgling and growing stronger every day. Yashoda loved to carry him on her hip while she did her chores. But one day as she swept the courtyard she said, "Either you are the heaviest baby on Earth or I am getting weak." She laid Krishna down to rest her weary back.

At that very moment a dust storm blew into the village. Dust stung Yashoda's eyes and blinded her. She groped around but could not find Krishna. She called out to him, but her voice was lost in the deafening roar of the storm.

This storm was actually the demon Trinavrata. Kansa had sent him to Gokul to find and kill Krishna. When he spotted the baby in Yashoda's courtyard he scooped him up and said, "Care to come for a ride, sonny?"

Krishna never refused a chance for fun. He flew happily into the sky on the spinning cloud of dust. But soon, just like Yashoda, the weary demon began to mumble, "Either you are the heaviest baby on Earth or I am getting weak." Krishna continued to grow heavier and heavier. Trinavrata could not carry him anymore, but Krishna would not let go. Holding fast to the demon's dusty beard, he said, "I am going down and you are going down with me, Trinavrata," Soon they both came tumbling from the dusty sky.

When the storm ended, a worried Yashoda called out, "Krishna, where are you?" She heard Krishna's joyful squeals and found him well and happy, exactly where she had left him just a few moments before. But next to him was the shattered body of a demon!

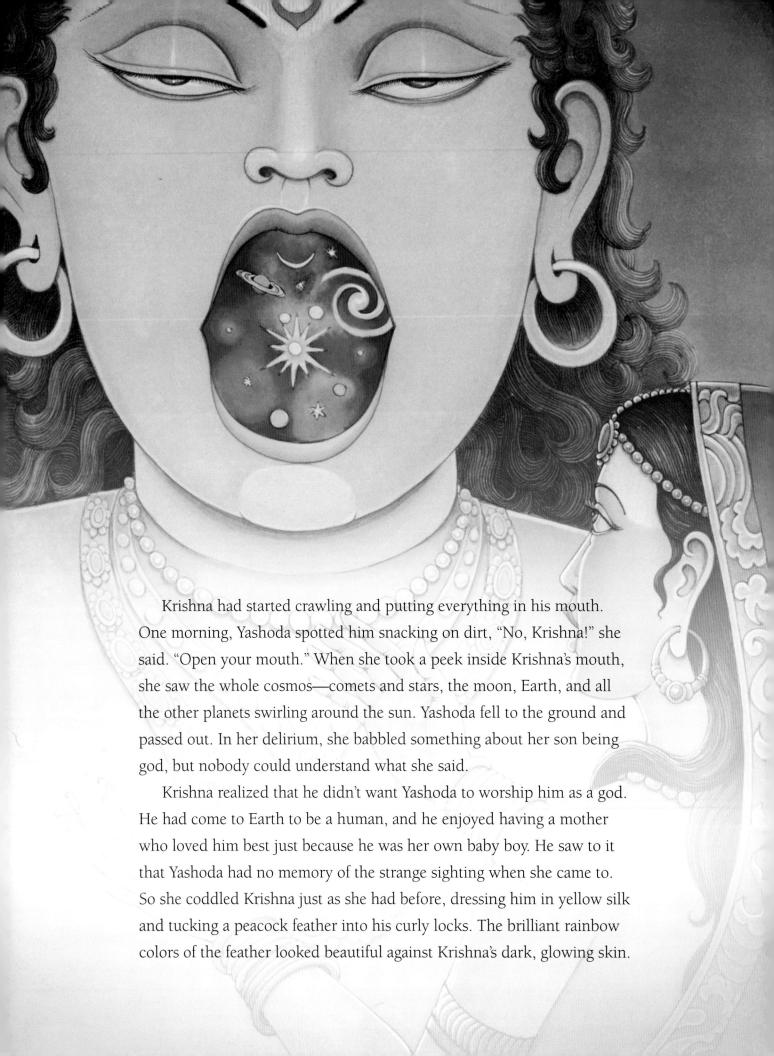

Krishna had started crawling and putting everything in his mouth. One morning, Yashoda spotted him snacking on dirt, "No, Krishna!" she said. "Open your mouth." When she took a peek inside Krishna's mouth, she saw the whole cosmos—comets and stars, the moon, Earth, and all the other planets swirling around the sun. Yashoda fell to the ground and passed out. In her delirium, she babbled something about her son being god, but nobody could understand what she said.

Krishna realized that he didn't want Yashoda to worship him as a god. He had come to Earth to be a human, and he enjoyed having a mother who loved him best just because he was her own baby boy. He saw to it that Yashoda had no memory of the strange sighting when she came to. So she coddled Krishna just as she had before, dressing him in yellow silk and tucking a peacock feather into his curly locks. The brilliant rainbow colors of the feather looked beautiful against Krishna's dark, glowing skin.

When he was just a little boy, Krishna's family moved from Gokul to the village of Vrindavan. When he grew a little older, Krishna joined the other village boys as they herded the cows out to pasture. As a toddler, he had developed a taste for fresh butter. Now he organized butter-stealing parties with his cowherd friends. Krishna and company would sneak into their neighbors' larders and help themselves to as much butter as they could eat.

The distraught neighbors came to Yashoda with their complaints.

"Your Krishna is a thief. He steals our butter and disappears."

"And he makes our cows disappear at milking time!"

"You must punish him, Yashoda. Do something!"

Yashoda tried to speak sternly to Krishna. But he would put on such an innocent smile and speak with such charm that she couldn't stay angry for long. When Krishna gave his mother an affectionate bear hug and protested, "Mother, you love me. You know I don't steal . . ." all of Yashoda's doubts and anger would fall from her like dry, old leaves from the trees. No complaint could make Yashoda love Krishna any less.

Soon, however, Krishna's fun with butter began costing the villagers their livelihoods. Every week they carried pots of butter on their heads to pay the tax collectors across the river in Mathura. But the tax collectors got nothing when Krishna and his friends hid in the trees and stole the butter pots right off the milkmaids' heads. The villagers complained to Kansa that Krishna ate up all their butter. Of course, that made Kansa furious. He turned to his demon crony Vatasura and ordered him to kill Krishna, exclaiming, "That boy must die!"

Vatasura turned himself into a calf and joined Krishna's herd. *When Krishna comes to pet me I will make a pulp out of him,* he thought. But Krishna noticed that one of the calves looked a bit too perfect, yet none of the cows would let him suckle. Curious, Krishna approached the calf and asked him, "Where is your mother?" The calf was waiting for just this moment. His features began to harden and he growled at Krishna. In a flash, Krishna grabbed the calf by his tail, spun him around above his head, and threw him up into the sky beyond the tree line. The calf landed with a thud among rocks and shrubs. He was no longer a cute little calf. Now he was a dead demon.

Next, Kansa sent the demon Bakasura to finish Krishna off. *I will make mincemeat out of Krishna with my sharp talons and beak*, thought Bakasura, as he turned himself into a bird and landed on the back of one of Krishna's cows. The cows grazed peacefully. A few birds rode on their backs, picking out ticks from time to time. But Krishna spotted a bird that seemed to be a little bit too alert, as if it was looking for someone. "Looks like you are from a different flock," Krishna said, and gently he lifted the bird off the cow's back. The demon bird was waiting for just this moment. He began pecking furiously at Krishna. Poor bird. Soon, his sharp beak was forced apart and instead of a bird, there lay Bakasura meeting his maker.

The demon Aghasura was full of rage. He wanted to avenge the death of his brother, Bakasura. "I will eat Krishna alive," he promised Kansa, and he turned himself into a huge serpent. With his mouth wide open, he lay coiled in the path that Krishna took when he herded his cows back to the village.

"You guys stay here. I need to see about this snake," Krishna said to his friends, as he marched gallantly into the serpent's gaping mouth. As Krishna ventured further in, the serpent's long stomach got narrower and narrower. "Okay, it's time for me to grow up," said Krishna, and he began to grow bigger and bigger and bigger, stretching the serpent's belly till it could stretch no more. Krishna's friends heard a noise that sounded as if the earth itself was tearing apart . . . and out from the torn flesh of the serpent stepped a smiling Krishna.

The story of Krishna's brave encounters with the demons made all of the young milkmaids fall in love with him. Each of them wanted Krishna for her husband. One day while the milkmaids were bathing in the river, Krishna happened to pass by. He spotted their clothes lying on the riverbank. Scooping them up, he climbed to the highest branch of a nearby tree and began playing his flute. When the girls heard his music, they wanted to come out of the river to meet him. But when they looked up, they saw their clothes hanging from the highest branches of the tree!

"Give us our clothes, Krishna," they begged.

"Come out of the river and get them," teased Krishna.

One by one, the girls came out of the river covering themselves with their hands as best as they could. Krishna cast a kind gaze upon each of them. As if by magic, the girls felt free of their romantic designs on Krishna. Now they felt only divine love in their hearts. "You are our Lord," they said. Krishna was very, very happy to be out from under so many marriage proposals.

Though naughty and full of mischief, Krishna was also very good at understanding how the human heart yearns for love. On one full-moon night, he began playing his flute. His divine music wafted into every home on the soft, floral-scented breeze, and from every home, out came the milkmaids. Tall and short, fat and thin, beautiful and ugly, dark and fair—not one of them could resist Krishna's enchanting music. Entranced, they made a beeline for the source of the melody. Soon every milkmaid found herself facing her very own Krishna, for Krishna had multiplied himself into many. "I am everywhere," he said. "To experience me, all you have to do is awaken pure love in your heart."

There was not a cloud in the sky. The milkmaids and Krishna danced and danced all night long, the moon shining brightly on their lovely faces. The rhythmic tapping of their feet and the rustling of their silky robes were the only other sounds besides the melody from Krishna's flute.

The real Krishna played and danced with his eternal sweetheart, Radha, just as he had promised Goddess Lakshmi in the Ksheer Sagar. Into her ear he whispered, "As long as the sun and the moon appear in the sky, our names will be chanted together."

It was a custom in those days, as the hot summer months were coming to an end, to pray to Lord Indra, ruler of the heavens and dispenser of rain, for life-giving rains to nourish the crops. It had not rained in a long time. The Yamuna River was running low. In places, the riverbed was dry. The cows grew thin and gaunt with no fresh grass to eat. But still, Lord Indra did not send the rains.

Krishna said, "The rains will come when the clouds have gathered enough water. Instead of flattering Indra, let us honor the wise men of our community." Lord Indra did not like all attention diverted from him. In a fury he sent a searing bolt of lightening followed by rain so hard it could peel skin off the body.

The villagers panicked, "O Narayana, save us from Lord Indra," they prayed. Krishna was none other than Narayana, and he always heard a call for help. He lifted Govardhan Mountain on his little pinky and held it up like an umbrella. The cattle and the villagers took shelter under the mountain. The battering rains continued on, but now no one cared. Humbled, Lord Indra appeared before Krishna and said, "Forgive me, Narayana." The rains became gentle and soft, and the happy villagers returned to their homes.

Kansa's demons had made many attempts on Krishna's life, but Krishna had killed them all without suffering so much as a scratch. This made Kansa very unhappy. He summoned Akrura, a great devotee of Lord Vishnu. "Akrura, my friend," said Kansa, "I regret that for years I have tried to kill my nephew Krishna. I would like to meet him. Please bring him here."

Akrura doubted Kansa's intentions, but he hitched two handsome horses to his wagon and headed toward Gokul, praying all the way, "Help us, Narayana." The villagers said, "Your cousin Balaram will go with you, Krishna. We will not let you go alone."

On the way to Mathura, the horses needed a drink. "Water the horses. We will wait in the carriage," Krishna said. Akrura watered the horses and hitched them back up. When he returned to the lake for a cooling swim, he saw an image in the water—Krishna reclined on a coiled serpent holding a conch shell, a mace, a lotus flower, and a discus in his hands. Akrura couldn't believe his eyes. He looked back at the wagon on the shore. Krishna and Balaram were sitting right where he had left them! He swam back to the shore and fell at Krishna's feet, crying, "You are Narayana, aren't you?"

"You must be seeing things," said Krishna. He hugged Akrura, and the devotee's heart filled with hope and love.

In Mathura, Kansa received Krishna and Balaram very warmly. He led the boys into a public arena and announced to the crowd, "Now, my nephews will play with elephants!" Kansa hoped that the elephants would crush the boys to death. But, the boys flattened the charging beasts as if they were children's toys. Pulling off the tusks, they waved to the cheering crowds.

Not one to give up, Kansa cried, "Krishna and Balaram will now take on my wrestlers!"

"Only two against so many . . . not fair," murmured the crowd. But Kansa ignored their protests and signaled for his bloodthirsty wrestlers to attack the boys. Krishna and Balaram slew the wrestlers in a matter of minutes. Humiliated, Kansa called his eight brothers for help. Again, Krishna and Balaram killed them with one sweep of their hands.

There was no one left on Kansa's side. "Well, *I* will crush these boys like bugs," he boasted, as he marched into the ring.

"You can deal with him, Krishna," said Balaram. He stood aside as Krishna gathered Kansa's hair in his hand, pulled his uncle's head back, and struck one fatal blow to his spine. The crowd could not believe that the reign of terror was over! They spilled over into the ring, lifted the boys onto their shoulders, and danced with joy.

The earth goddess, Bhumi, sighed with relief. "Thank you, Narayana, for fulfilling your promise," she said with gratitude.

Soon after, Krishna and Balaram headed to the prison to meet with Devaki, Vasudeva, and King Ugrasena. Krishna's parents hugged him with joy.

To the late Kansa's father, Krishna said, "Grandfather, now you'll have a chance to undo all of Kansa's evil deeds."

"I am old, my child," said Ugrasena. "You deserve to be the king."

"Not me!" cried Krishna. "I'd rather herd my beloved cows than be a king and live in a palace." Once Grandfather Ugrasena was crowned and Krishna's parents had been set free, Krishna and Balaram returned to Gokul.

Krishna could escape being a king for the time being, but he could not escape going to school. He was sent to the ashram of Rishi Sandeepani, where he spent years learning how to become a warrior king. All that training would help him keep his promise to mankind, "Anytime the earth is overrun with evil, I will come to restore peace and order."

A Note to Parents and Teachers

At its heart, Krishna's story is the story of a child wanting pure love from his mother. Though he is a divine incarnation, born with unparalleled strength and magical powers, he doesn't want to be worshipped as a god. He wants only to be loved as a human child. His story points to the primal need of all children. Receiving love from parents and community is a child's birthright. When given unconditionally, it allows the child to develop his or her true potential as an adult.

The Hindu worldview recognizes nine primary emotional states, or rasas. They are both positive and negative, ranging from love, bravery, and tranquillity to fear, disgust, and anger. In India small children are encouraged to express the full range of emotions in order to become fully developed human beings. Small children are considered innocent, even godlike, so even their negative emotional expressions are seen only as opportunities to give them the love they need. An Indian mother will call her child "Krishna" as a reminder that innocence and trust are the true powers that children bring into the world.

About the Illustrations

Pieter Weltevrede created the illustrations with watercolor and tempera paints. Using the transparent watercolors, the artist painted each picture in several steps. After outlining the figures, he filled them in, using three tones for each color to achieve a three-dimensional effect; next he applied the background colors. After each step he "fixed" the painting by rinsing it with water until only the paint absorbed by the paper remained.

Then the artist applied a "wash," using the opaque tempera paints. After wetting the painting again, he applied the tempera to the surface until the whole painting appeared to be behind a colored fog. While the wash color was still wet, he used a dry brush to remove it from the faces, hands, and feet of the figures. He let the wash dry completely, then rinsed it again to fix the colors. To achieve the desired color and emotional tone, each painting received several washes and fixes. Finally, the artist redefined the delicate line work of each piece, allowing the painting to reemerge from within the clouds of wash.

Please feel free to trace or photocopy this line drawing of Krishna for children to color.